DRESSAGE

Rosie Heywood
Designed by Ian McNee

Illustrated by Mikki Rain
Photographs by Kit Houghton
Consultants: Juliet Mander BHSII,
Moira Harris

Series Editor: Felicity Brooks
Managing Designer: Mary Cartwright
Additional designs by Susannah Owen

Contents

WHAT IS DRESSAGE?

Dressage is a method of training your horse and improving your riding skills so that you and your horse work well together and understand each other clearly. With practice, dressage should make your horse supple so that his movements remain flowing when you ride him. It should also help to make him more confident and eager to please you.

STARTING DRESSAGE

When horses are out in the field, they move with light, easy steps. The goal of dressage is to maintain these flowing movements.

You can start to learn dressage at any time. It doesn't matter how long you've been riding, or how experienced you are. In fact, you learn some basic skills of dressage, such as how to sit in the saddle correctly, when you first start to ride.

Dressage movements are designed to make your horse strong, supple and balanced. As you continue dressage training, the movements gradually become more challenging for you and your horse.

Although dressage does not involve jumping or riding at high speed, it improves your accuracy and control, which will help with all your other riding activities.

THE HISTORY OF DRESSAGE

The art of teaching horses to obey their riders willingly was first practiced by the ancient Greeks over two thousand years ago. In the 16th century, riding schools in Europe trained noblemen in the art of horsemanship. Cavalry horses were taught difficult movements which would frighten enemies in battle. Displays of these impressive skills became popular.

In 1735, the Spanish Riding School opened in Vienna, Austria. Modern dressage developed from the teachings of this famous school. The Spanish Riding School is still based in Vienna and its riders and horses continue to perform all over the world.

This horse and rider from the Spanish Riding School are performing a movement called the capriole which was originally used in battle.

DRESSAGE SHOWS

Taking part in a dressage show is a great way to see how well you and your horse are progressing. It also gives you the chance to watch other horses and riders of different levels. Dressage is becoming a popular sport, and there are plenty of competitions and levels to choose from.

Advanced horses and riders make complicated dressage movements look easy, but it takes years of training to reach such a high standard.

POINTS OF A HORSE

The different parts of a horse's body are called the "points." These terms are often used in dressage, so it's important to know what they mean.

Poll · Neck · Withers · Girth · Croup · Shoulder · Hindquarters (quarters) · Forehand (front legs) · Hindlegs (back legs) · Near foreleg · Hock · Knee · Near hindleg · Off foreleg · Off hindleg · Fetlock · Pastern

YOUR POSITION

Developing your riding position is an important part of
becoming a dressage rider. A good position will help your
horse keep his balance and make it easier for him to move
naturally. Although there's a lot to think about when you
work on your position, try to stay relaxed.

ACHIEVING A GOOD POSITION

It takes practice to achieve a good
riding position. Even experienced
dressage riders continue to work on
this part of their riding. Try
to sit tall and balanced
in the saddle. If you are
sitting crookedly, your horse
will find it hard to keep his
body straight. Ask someone
to watch you while you ride.
They can then pinpoint any
problems you may not be
aware of. This rider has a
good position.

Her head is up and she is looking straight ahead.

Her shoulders are level.

Her back is straight but not stiff.

Her elbows are bent and flexible.

She is sitting in the center of the saddle, with her weight evenly spread between her seat bones.

Her knees are resting gently against the saddle flaps.

Her upper legs or thighs are relaxed.

Her lower legs are in contact with the horse, next to the girth.

Her heels are lower than her toes.

Her feet are pointing forward. The balls of her feet are resting on the stirrup bars.

RIDING WITH LONGER STIRRUPS

Dressage riders lengthen
their stirrups so that they
can ride with longer legs.
Riding with longer legs
means more of your leg is
in contact with your horse's
sides. This helps you to
give lighter, clearer leg aids
(see page 6). You'll need
to have good balance
before you start to ride with
longer stirrups.

Your stirrups should be two holes longer than normal. There should be a vertical straight line from your hip to your heel.

In contrast, short stirrups are used for jumping. They help you to lean forward, so your weight is off your horse's back.

IMPROVING YOUR POSITION

One of the best ways to improve your riding position is to have some longe-line lessons. The instructor controls your horse with a longe-line, while you concentrate on keeping a good position. You can also practice riding without reins or without stirrups in longe-line lessons. Riding without stirrups is good practice for dressage, as it helps you to prepare for lengthened stirrups.

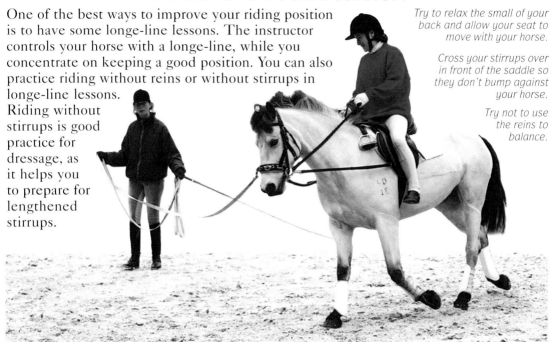

Try to relax the small of your back and allow your seat to move with your horse.

Cross your stirrups over in front of the saddle so they don't bump against your horse.

Try not to use the reins to balance.

Working without stirrups will improve your balance so that you don't have to depend on reins or stirrups to help keep your position.

EXERCISES ON THE LONGE-LINE

There are lots of exercises you can do on the longe-line. The ones described here will loosen your muscles and joints so that you don't become stiff. They will also help to make you more supple, so that you can absorb your horse's cantering and trotting motion through your seat, hips and back. Working on the longe-line can be tiring at first, so make sure that you and your horse take frequent breaks.

Put your arms out to the sides and swing around to face each side. Try to keep your legs still. Then do the exercise at a trot, with your hands on your hips.

Keep your feet in the stirrups. Hold the pommel with one hand. Lift your other arm in the air. Swing it backward in a circle. Repeat with the other arm.

Take your feet out of the stirrups. Bend one leg until you can hold your foot with your hand. Stretch your thigh so your knee points down, then straighten.

USING THE AIDS

You can give signals to your horse which tell him what you want him to do. These signals are called aids, and you give them by using your hands, legs, seat and voice. You can also use artificial aids such as whips and spurs. In dressage, your aids must be as clear and light as you can make them, so that your horse can understand you quickly and easily.

USING YOUR LEGS

To give leg aids, your legs should be relaxed, with your lower legs in contact with your horse's sides. You use leg aids to ask your horse to move ahead, to keep him working energetically and to tell him where to go. The message you give him depends on where you put your legs and how firmly you use them. To move straight forward, use both legs near the girth. To bend, keep your inside leg at the girth, and your outside leg behind it.

This rider's aids tell her horse to bend to the right. Her legs are well positioned, but her left shoulder and arm should be further forward.

Outside leg

HAND AIDS

You can use your hands to send signals to your horse along the reins to his mouth. Always try to keep the feeling with his mouth soft and light. Squeeze your fingers on the reins to slow him down. If you pull hard on your horse's mouth he may start to ignore or resist your hand aids.

Use the inside rein to ask for a bend toward the inside.

Use the outside rein to control your horse's bend and speed.

Inside leg

Your outside leg is the one nearest the outside of the arena or circle. You use it to control your horse's hindquarters.

Your inside leg is the one nearest to the middle of the arena or circle. You use it to ask your horse to bend toward the inside and move with energy.

Tips for giving aids
- To give clear aids you must have good balance, and be in a correct position.
- If your horse does not respond, check that you are giving the correct aids.
- Try to keep your hands, legs and seat still when you are not using them.
- Try to use your aids as sensitively as possible, so that your horse remains responsive to you.
- Try not to give your horse conflicting aids such as pulling on the reins when you are using your legs to ask him to move forward.

SEAT AIDS

Your seat and body can be used to slow
your horse down. On a correctly trained
horse, they can also be used to create more
energy and to ask your horse to bring his
hindlegs farther underneath him. Your
seat and body should be in balance
with your horse, so don't
tip forward
or backward.

*To slow your horse
down, sit tall, with
your weight down
into your heels.*

*Try to sit still. If
you move around,
your horse may
become confused.*

USING YOUR VOICE

You're not allowed to use your voice
in dressage tests, but you can use it
to reinforce other aids while you're
training. Your horse understands
the way you say words, rather than
the words themselves. Quick, high-
pitched commands will keep him
moving, while slow, low-pitched
commands will slow him down.

DRESSAGE WHIPS

If your horse ignores your leg aids, you can use a whip to
emphasize what you mean. Give your horse the correct leg
aid first. If he doesn't respond, tap him with the whip just
behind your leg. If you're using a standard crop, put the
reins in one hand, so you can use the other hand to apply
the whip without pulling on the reins.

Standard crop

Dressage whip

*Dressage whips are longer than
standard crops, so you can
use them without taking
your hands off the reins.*

*Hold your whip in
your inside hand.*

SPURS

Spurs are worn by
experienced dressage
riders to give light leg aids.
Riders only start to use
spurs when they have
developed a good leg
position and are able to
keep their legs still, so that
the spurs never touch the
horse by mistake.

*The shank of the spur should be no
longer than 3cm (1in).*

*Only blunt spurs can be worn in US
Pony Club dressage tests.*

THE GAITS

Your horse can walk, trot, canter and gallop. These different steps are called his gaits. In dressage tests, you will be asked to show how well your horse moves in each gait, except gallop. Before you can begin to improve your horse's gaits you will need to understand how he moves in each one.

MOVEMENTS IN WALK

Your horse walks by moving his legs one at a time. On a hard surface, you should be able to hear four separate sounds, called beats, as each hoof hits the ground. His back hooves should step into the marks left by his front hooves. This is called "tracking up." With training, his hindlegs should "over-track" and step over the hoof prints from his forelegs. If a horse moves two legs at the same time, he is gaiting rather than walking. This is a serious fault. A horse may gait if he wasn't trained properly when he was young, or if his rider keeps the reins too short.

Beat one   *Beat two*   *Beat three*   *Beat four*

Off (right) hindleg hits the ground.   *Off foreleg*   *Near (left) hindleg*   *Near foreleg*

MOVEMENTS IN TROT

When your horse trots, he moves his legs in diagonal pairs. As he springs from one pair of legs to the other, there is a moment when all his legs are off the ground. This is called "the moment of suspension." Your horse's trot should have a regular rhythm and his hindlegs should track up into the hoof prints of his forelegs. The speed of your horse's trot is important. If he trots too fast, he won't have time for the moment of suspension. If he's too slow, he will start to drag his feet.

Beat one   *Beat two*

Off hindleg   *Near foreleg*   *Near hindleg*   *Off foreleg*

The horse's off hindleg and near foreleg hit the ground at the same time.

All the horse's legs are in the air for the moment of suspension.

His near hindleg and off foreleg then hit the ground at the same time.

Another moment of suspension follows, then the sequence is repeated.

CANTER

There should be three quick beats to your horse's canter, followed by a moment of suspension when all his feet are off the ground. Your horse should canter with even strides. Most of his weight should be on his haunches, and he should step well under his body. A lazy horse may lose the moment of suspension or move his inside hindleg and outside foreleg separately instead of together.

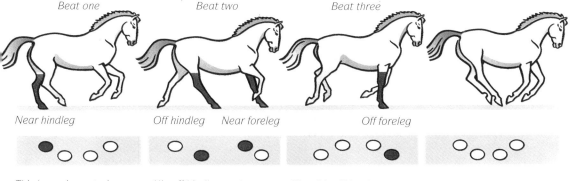

Beat one   *Beat two*   *Beat three*

Near hindleg   *Off hindleg*   *Near foreleg*   *Off foreleg*

This horse is cantering on the right leg. He pushes off with his near hindleg.

His off hindleg and near foreleg hit the ground at the same time.

Then his off foreleg steps forward and hits the ground.

All his legs leave the ground for the moment of suspension.

DIFFERENT TYPES OF WALK, TROT AND CANTER

Dressage horses can vary the length of their steps in each gait without changing their speed. It's hard work for horses to shorten or lengthen their strides and it takes careful training. The ultimate shortened and lengthened gaits are called "collected" and "extended." You can learn about them on pages 16 and 17.

This horse is stretching his neck well forward for the free walk.

In medium trot, the horse stretches out his body to take longer steps.

Walks

Your horse's normal walk is called "medium walk." In lower level dressage tests you may also be asked to show "free walk." For free walk, give your horse a long, but not completely loose, rein so he can stretch out his back and neck and take longer steps. He should move forward actively, without slowing down.

Trots and canters

Your horse's normal trot and canter are called his "working" trot and canter. In lower level dressage tests you will have to show that your horse can take slightly longer steps than in his working gaits. This is the first stage toward "medium" trot and canter, in which your horse lengthens his stride.

WAY OF GOING

A horse's "way of going" describes the way he moves. If your horse is moving along and working correctly he will be feeling relaxed and happy. You will also find him comfortable to ride. Here are some important points which will affect your horse's way of going.

KEEPING YOUR HORSE STRAIGHT

Your horse should be able to keep straight in all his gaits. This means that his hindlegs should follow in the tracks of his forelegs and not swing out to the sides. His body should be straight from the tip of his nose to his tail, or gently curved if you are riding a circle. If your horse isn't straight, it may be because you are riding crookedly, or because you have stronger contact on one rein.

This horse has started to shift his body to the right because his rider is sitting crookedly.

It could also be because your horse is not responding to your aids properly. Longeing exercises (see page 5) will help you to sit straight, while transitions (see page 12) will help to make your horse "listen" to your aids. Practice riding straight lines across the arena so that your horse doesn't start to rely on the rail or fence of the arena to keep himself straight.

STAYING CORRECTLY BALANCED

To be correctly balanced, your horse must be moving forward actively (with lively steps) in response to your aids. He must be working with plenty of impulsion (see next page) from his hindquarters. If he starts to rush, he may lose his rhythm and put more weight on his forehand. He may lean against the reins to balance, and he'll be more likely to trip. A horse who is well balanced is said to be in "self carriage."

Rhythm and tempo
- Rhythm is the regularity of your horse's hoof beats. When his rhythm is steady, his balance will be good.
- Tempo is the speed of your horse's rhythm. In dressage, your horse's tempo should stay constant.

Hillwork when you're out on the trail is an excellent way to improve your horse's balance.

CREATING IMPULSION

Impulsion is the energy your horse uses to move forward. When you use your aids to control this energy, your horse will take lighter, springier steps. His hocks will engage, which means he'll put more of his weight onto his hindquarters and use his hindlegs to push himself along. His hindlegs will step further underneath his body.

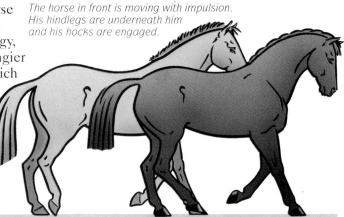

The horse in front is moving with impulsion. His hindlegs are underneath him and his hocks are engaged.

The hocks of the horse behind are not engaged.

ACCEPTING THE BIT

When your horse accepts the bit, he will move forward until he can feel a light but steady pressure, called contact, between the reins and the bit. You will be able to feel this contact too. There should be no resistance to the bit felt in his mouth, neck or back. His frame (the shape his body makes) should become rounder. A horse won't accept the bit until he is straight, balanced and moving with impulsion.

This horse has accepted the bit and his outline is well rounded. His back and loins are supple and relaxed.

The horse's neck is gently curved from the withers to the poll and his jaw is relaxed.

This horse is not accepting the bit. His outline is "hollow" and his ears are back as a sign of resistance.

His tail is soft and swinging.

Helping your horse to accept the bit
- Use your legs to push your horse firmly forward.
- Keep your hands still.
- Don't try to create contact by pulling on the reins.
- As soon as your horse accepts the bit, relax your aids slightly to reward him.

TRANSITIONS

A transition is a change of gait, such as from walk to trot, or from working trot to medium trot. Transitions teach your horse to pay attention to your aids and help to improve his balance and impulsion. They are included in all levels of dressage, from Introductory to Grand Prix.

UPWARD TRANSITIONS

Upward transitions increase the pace, for example, from walk to trot. Before you ask for an upward transition, make sure your horse is attentive and moving energetically.

Sit lightly in the saddle. Close your legs on your horse's sides by the girth. Follow his head movements with your hands but don't lose contact with his mouth.

Walk

Let your body move forward with your horse. This will help you to balance in the next gait.

Trot

UPWARD TRANSITION TO CANTER

Your horse should canter with his inside leg leading. Go into sitting trot before you ask for canter. Use your inside leg on the girth and your outside leg behind the girth. This tells your horse to start, or "strike off," with his outside hindleg, so that his inside foreleg leads the canter (see page 9). Asking for canter as you go around a corner will encourage your horse to start with the correct leg.

DOWNWARD TRANSITIONS

Don't pull on the reins to slow your horse down. It's uncomfortable for him.

This horse is cantering with the correct, inside leg leading.

Downward transitions slow the pace. To ask for one, sit taller in the saddle, with your weight down in your heels. Keep your legs lightly on your horse's sides. Close your fingers around the reins and squeeze, as if you were squeezing a sponge.

DOWNWARD TRANSITION TO HALT

When your horse halts, he should stand straight and square. This means that he has equal weight on each leg, and that his front and back legs are in line. He should be able to keep still, without fidgeting or shuffling around. Keep a light rein contact during the halt, so that he stays alert, waiting for your next command.

Stepping back

Crooked halt

Resisting

Don't try to force your horse to stop by pulling the reins.

If your horse steps back, it may be because your hand aids are too strong. Loosen your rein contact as soon as he stops, but don't let the reins go loose.

If your horse's halt is crooked, make sure your left and right aids are even. Try placing two poles on the ground and halting between them.

If your horse resists the halt, it may be because your aids were unclear, or because your horse was not moving well before the halt. Try to use clear aids.

USING THE HALF-HALT

In dressage tests you will be asked to change gait at specific markers. Giving a half-halt is a good way to prepare your horse for transitions.

This rider should have a little more weight in her heels.

A half-halt is a set of aids which alert your horse that you're about to ask him to do something different, such as change gait. It also tells him to engage his hindquarters and hocks. Half-halts can be used in all gaits, but practice in trot first. Sit tall in the saddle and put your weight into the stirrups. Close your legs around your horse's sides (telling him to go forward) and close your fingers on the reins so that they restrain him.

B

CIRCLES AND TURNS

Dressage tests consist of a series of circles, turns and transitions. These movements are designed to show off your horse's ability and training. More advanced dressage tests involve smaller circles and tighter turns. With regular practice, your horse's suppleness and balance will improve so that you can start to ride smaller, more precise shapes.

HOW A DRESSAGE HORSE BENDS

When a horse bends correctly, he curves his whole body, from his tail to his poll (the top of his head). His outside hindleg steps into the same track as his outside foreleg, while his inside hindleg steps well underneath his body. He is well balanced, his rhythm and tempo stay the same and his body has a rounded outline. He looks in the direction he's going and doesn't bend his neck towards the outside.

This horse is bending correctly. His whole body is bending along the curve of the circle.

This horse is bending incorrectly. His shoulders are "falling-out" from the curve of the circle.

AIDS FOR BENDING

Keep your head up and look in the direction you are going.

To help your horse keep his balance, turn your body so that your shoulders are in line with his shoulders.

To encourage your horse to bend his whole body, use your inside leg on the girth. Use your outside leg behind the girth to control his hindquarters. Squeeze and release the inside rein to make sure your horse bends his neck. Use your outside hand to control his speed and stop his neck bending too much.

Your horse may be stiff on one side and find it harder to bend that way. You will need to work this stiff side a little harder to loosen it. Start your training sessions with circles on his easier side before you change to his stiffer side.

Bending terms

A change of direction is called a change of rein.

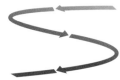

A circle or bend to the right (in a clockwise direction) is called a circle or bend on the right rein.

A circle or bend to the left (in a counter-clockwise direction) is called a circle or bend on the left rein.

14

RIDING CIRCLES IN THE ARENA

The picture below shows how a small dressage arena is laid out. Letters are placed at specific points around the outside. Because they are in the centre, the letters D, G and X are not marked in the arena. When you ride a test, you will be asked to begin each circle at a particular letter. You may be asked to ride a 20m (66ft) circle, a 15m (49ft) circle, or a 10m (33ft) circle, which is the most advanced.

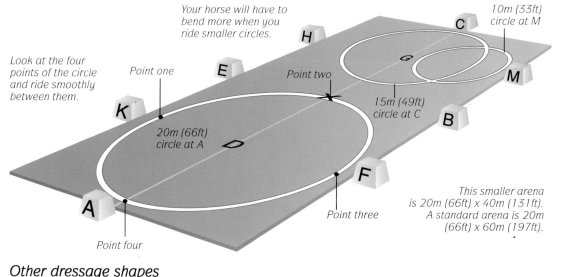

Your horse will have to bend more when you ride smaller circles.

Look at the four points of the circle and ride smoothly between them.

Point one

Point two

10m (33ft) circle at M

15m (49ft) circle at C

20m (66ft) circle at A

Point three

Point four

This smaller arena is 20m (66ft) x 40m (131ft). A standard arena is 20m (66ft) x 60m (197ft).

Other dressage shapes

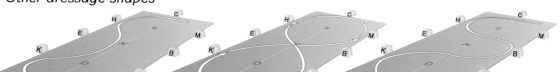

Shallow loops involve a slight bend.   *Figures-of-eight change your direction.*   *Serpentines are a series of loops.*

TURNS IN THE ARENA

In dressage, a bend from one straight line to another is called a turn. You will need to plan ahead in order to ride accurately. The most difficult turn is onto the centerline. Practice riding it from both directions.

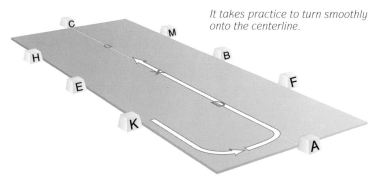

It takes practice to turn smoothly onto the centerline.

Centerline turns

• Look down the centreline before you start to turn onto it.

• Ride the turn with an even bend, then straighten up by using equal rein and leg contact on your horse's sides.

• Look ahead and sit in the center of the saddle.

• If your horse drifts left, use your left leg to push him back to the center.

COLLECTING AND EXTENDING

Dressage horses can take longer or shorter steps in each gait, while keeping the same rhythm and tempo. This is called extending and collecting. You can start to collect and extend when, as a result of transition and circle work, your horse has become supple, balanced and responsive. Walk is the hardest pace to collect or extend, so begin training in trot and canter.

COLLECTED GAITS

In collected gaits, the horse takes shorter, higher steps. He covers less ground with each step, so that in trot and canter, the moment of suspension is more pronounced. The movement of the gait has an upward, rather than a forward, feel. The rider stays in sitting trot.

Most of the horse's weight is on his hindquarters, so that his forelegs are "light."

His hocks are well engaged and his outline is rounded.

This horse is in a good collected trot. The rider is well positioned and is sitting lightly in the saddle.

The horse's head is almost vertical.

His neck is raised and arched.

He is bending his legs well to make his steps higher.

WORKING TOWARDS COLLECTION

Your horse will be expected to show the first stages of collection in lower level dressage tests. At each test above First Level, a greater degree of collection will be required.

It's difficult for your horse to collect his gaits. Ask him to shorten his steps for a few strides at first, then push him into his working gait.

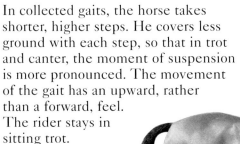

The aids for collection

- Close your legs around your horse's sides so that he moves forward with impulsion.
- At the same time, close your fingers on the reins to contain your horse's forward movement.
- Listen to your horse's rhythm and tempo. They should stay the same.

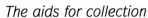

Small circles are good training for collection.

EXTENDED GAITS

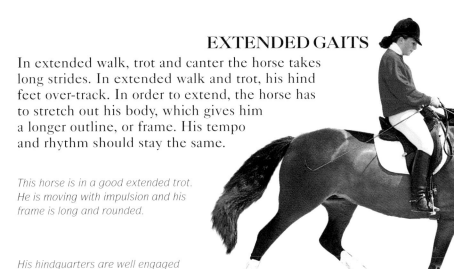

In extended walk, trot and canter the horse takes long strides. In extended walk and trot, his hind feet over-track. In order to extend, the horse has to stretch out his body, which gives him a longer outline, or frame. His tempo and rhythm should stay the same.

This horse is in a good extended trot. He is moving with impulsion and his frame is long and rounded.

His hindquarters are well engaged and he is light on his feet.

LEARNING TO EXTEND

Try extending in trot first. Use posting trot at first, as this will encourage your horse to take longer steps. Collect your horse's trot on the short side of the arena then use the extending aids (see below) as you go up the long side. Only ask for four or five lengthened strides at first, so he doesn't lose his balance, or start to take faster, shorter steps.

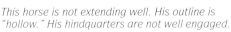

This horse is not extending well. His outline is "hollow." His hindquarters are not well engaged.

The aids to extend

* Use your legs to make your horse move with more impulsion.
* Let your hands follow the movement of his head and neck, so that he can lengthen his frame.
* Don't let the reins go loose, or he'll go faster.

* Make sure his rhythm and tempo stay the same in the extended gait.
* Only ask for a few extended steps at first.
* Work toward medium trot (see page 9) before you ask your horse to fully extend his trot.

COUNTING STRIDES

You can check whether your horse is extending and collecting by counting his strides. Count the number of strides he takes between two markers in working trot and canter. Ride between the markers again, asking your horse for collection or extension. Count his strides in each gait.

Horses should take more strides when they collect and fewer strides when they extend.

Your horse's rhythm and tempo should stay the same.

LATERAL WORK

In lateral work, a dressage horse moves his body sideways, so that his hindfeet do not follow in the tracks of his forefeet. There are several different lateral movements, some of which are included in dressage tests. Others are not included in tests, but are useful training exercises for you and your horse.

TURN ON THE FOREHAND

To do a turn on the forehand, a horse moves his hindlegs around to the side, while his forelegs stay in the same place. He should keep the same sequence of footfalls as in walk (see page 8), so that his forelegs mark time on the spot. His hindlegs should cross over each other as he moves them. Turn on the forehand is not asked for in tests, but it's a good introduction to lateral work.

Start with a quarter (90°) turn. Build up to a half (180°) turn, as shown here.

Aids for turn on the forehand
● Turn into the middle of the arena and establish a good halt.
● Use your inside leg firmly at the girth to ask your horse to move his hindquarters to the side.
● Keep your outside leg lightly behind the girth.
● Use your inside rein to encourage your horse to look towards the inside.
● Use your outside rein at the same time as your inside leg, to stop your horse from moving forward.

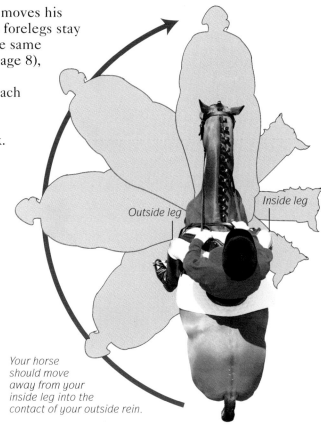

Outside leg

Inside leg

Your horse should move away from your inside leg into the contact of your outside rein.

POSSIBLE PROBLEMS

If your horse walks forward, face the edge of the arena when you practice.

If your horse resists your aids, he may need more practice at circles and turns, or your aids may be unclear. If he starts to step back, use firmer leg aids, and lighten your hand aids.

　　If he walks forward, you may be asking for too many steps too early, or your aids may be incorrect. If he bends his neck too much, lighten the inside rein and use the outside rein to control the amount of bend.

TURN ON THE HAUNCHES

To do a turn on the haunches, a horse moves his forelegs in a half circle around his hindlegs. He begins from a collected walk and puts his weight on his hindquarters to move his forelegs. Turn on the haunches is harder for a horse than turn on the forehand.

Give your horse a half-halt before you give him the aids for turn on the haunches. Ask for a quarter turn at first. It's better if your horse makes a small half circle with his hindlegs rather than stepping back, which is a serious fault.

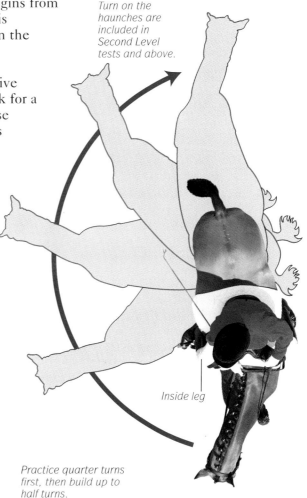

Turn on the haunches are included in Second Level tests and above.

Your horse's body should bend slightly in the direction he's going.

When you have completed the movement, always walk your horse forwards.

Aids for turn on the haunches
* Half-halt to collect your horse's walk.
* Use your inside leg at the girth to maintain inside bend and impulsion.
* Use your outside leg behind the girth to control your horse's hindquarters.
* Use the inside rein to ask your horse to bend toward the inside.
* Use the outside rein to control his speed and stop him from moving forward.
* Use the outside rein close to your horse's neck and the inside rein away from it to encourage him to move his forehand around.

Inside leg

Practice quarter turns first, then build up to half turns.

COMMON FAULTS

If your horse's quarters swing out to the side, use your outside leg more firmly to control them.

Outside leg

If your horse stops moving his inside hindleg or loses the correct sequence of footfalls, use your inside leg to increase his impulsion. Don't ask for too many steps at first, and walk him forward when you finish the movement.

If he steps back, you may be using too much outside rein. If he doesn't bend his body, ask for more bend in preparation, and use more inside leg and inside rein.

LEARNING TO LEG-YIELD

In leg-yield, a horse moves forward and diagonally sideways at the same time. His body should be straight, apart from his head, which should bend slightly away from the direction he's travelling in.

The leg-yield is used in First Level tests and it's a useful exercise because it teaches your horse obedience and balance. It also helps you to co-ordinate your aids and use them sensitively.

Aids for leg-yielding

• Use your inside leg firmly at the girth to move your horse sideways.
• Use your outside leg gently behind the girth to move him forward and stop his hindquarters from swinging out to the side.
• Use the inside rein gently to ask your horse for a slight inside bend at his poll.
• Use the outside rein firmly to steady your horse.
• Keep your weight in the center of the saddle. Try to stay in a balanced position.

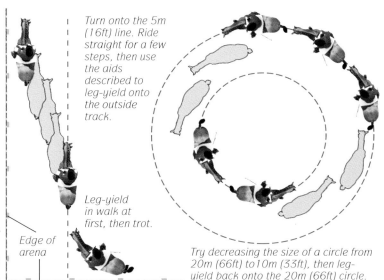

Turn onto the 5m (16ft) line. Ride straight for a few steps, then use the aids described to leg-yield onto the outside track.

Leg-yield in walk at first, then trot.

Edge of arena

Try decreasing the size of a circle from 20m (66ft) to 10m (33ft), then leg-yield back onto the 20m (66ft) circle.

SOLVING LEG-YIELDING PROBLEMS

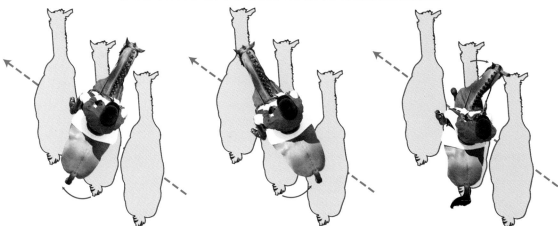

If your horse leads with his quarters, he probably lacks impulsion. Ensure you are riding straight before you ask for leg-yield, and ride him firmly forward.

If your pony trails his quarters and leads with his shoulders, use more outside rein. Use your inside leg further back to push his quarters over.

If he bends his neck too much, ease the contact with the inside rein. Ride him forward with plenty of impulsion to keep him straight in the leg-yield.

WHAT IS SHOULDER-IN?

When riding shoulder-in, a horse moves forward, with his body bent away from the direction he's travelling in. You'll be asked to ride shoulder-in in Second Level dressage tests and above. Shoulder-in will encourage your horse to engage his inside hindleg, making it easier for him to learn collection (see page 16).

When a horse performs shoulder-in, he makes three separate tracks with his feet.

His inside foreleg makes one track.

His inside hindleg and outside foreleg make a second track.

His outside hindleg makes a third track.

Edge of the arena

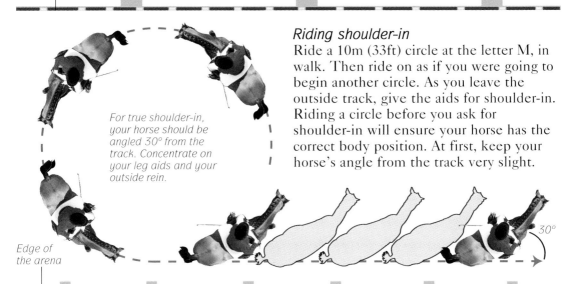

For true shoulder-in, your horse should be angled 30° from the track. Concentrate on your leg aids and your outside rein.

Edge of the arena

Riding shoulder-in

Ride a 10m (33ft) circle at the letter M, in walk. Then ride on as if you were going to begin another circle. As you leave the outside track, give the aids for shoulder-in. Riding a circle before you ask for shoulder-in will ensure your horse has the correct body position. At first, keep your horse's angle from the track very slight.

Aids for shoulder-in

● Use your inside leg at the girth to ask your horse to turn his body toward the inside.
● Use your outside leg behind the girth to prevent his quarters from swinging outwards.
● Use the inside rein very gently to reinforce the amount of bend.
● Use the outside rein to control the amount of bend and the speed.

Common problems with shoulder-in

● If your horse lacks impulsion, use your inside leg more firmly and check that he has not bent inward too much.
● If your horse varies the amount he bends, check you have the right balance between your inside leg and outside rein.
● If he is bending his neck too much, use more outside rein and less inside rein.
● If his quarters fall out, use your outside leg more firmly to control them.

21

EXERCISES IN CANTER

In lower level dressage, your horse should canter with his inside foreleg leading. This is known as "true canter" or being "on the correct leg." If you change the rein (see page 14), you must ask your horse to change his leading leg, so that he stays in true canter. Your horse's true canter should be well balanced on both reins.

WALK TO CANTER, CANTER TO WALK

This horse and rider are practising walk to canter and canter to walk transitions.

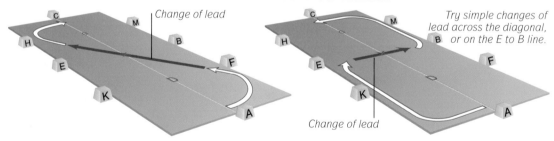

Transitions are good preparation for simple changes of leg (see below).

For walk to canter, make sure your horse has plenty of impulsion. Ride a 10m (33ft) circle as preparation. This will help your horse to engage his inside hindleg and help you to place your aids correctly. Use clear, firm canter aids when you are ready for the transition.

For canter to walk, ride a couple of steps of trot before you walk. This is called a progressive transition. Collect the canter first and keep your lower legs on your horse's sides to maintain the collection and impulsion. Use light hand aids when you ask for the transition.

SIMPLE CHANGE OF LEAD

Change of lead

Try simple changes of lead across the diagonal, or on the E to B line.

Change of lead

A "simple change of lead" is when a horse changes his leading leg in canter by trotting (or when more advanced, walking) for a few steps, then cantering again with his other leg leading. To ride a simple change of lead, use the canter aids (see page 12) to canter. To change your horse's lead, ask him to trot for three or four strides. Then use the canter aids again, but with your other leg behind the girth.

Possible problems
● If your horse resists your aids, he may not be ready for simple changes. Practice general transition work.
● If your horse pulls on the bit or trots faster, try simple changes on the E to B line so he has less room to speed up.
● If your horse canters with one leg leading in front and the opposite behind he is "disunited." Go back to walk or trot.

BEGINNING COUNTER CANTER

Counter canter is the opposite of true canter. The horse uses his outside leg to lead, with his body slightly bent towards the leading leg. He needs to be obedient, so he resists his natural impulse to lead with the inside leg. Counter canter will improve a horse's suppleness and balance, because he'll have to use different muscle combinations. Try the exercises below to introduce him to this difficult movement.

Counter canter

Counter canter

Begin by cantering with the inside leg leading. As you reach the long side of the arena, ride a shallow loop. When your horse turns back into the outside track he will be counter cantering for a few strides.

This dressage rider is performing a balanced, steady counter canter.

As his balance improves, canter a 15m (49ft) half circle at the end of the arena. Turn back on the track, so that your horse is in counter canter. Maintain counter canter to the quarter marker.

Keeping balanced
If your horse breaks into a trot or changes his leading leg, he may have lost his balance. Here's how to prevent this.
- Introduce your horse to counter canter gradually.
- Ride shallow loops smoothly.
- Try not to move suddenly in the saddle.
- As you turn back towards the outside track, keep your aids the same.

SADDLERY AND DRESS

When you enter a dressage test, read the rule book carefully to find out what you and your horse should wear. On the day, groom your horse thoroughly, and check that your clothes are clean and tidy. Knowing that you both look your best will boost your confidence when you enter the arena.

WHAT TO WEAR FOR DRESSAGE TESTS

This saddlery and dress should be suitable for most Pony Club and Lower Level tests, but always double-check in the relevant rule book.

Plain, leather snaffle bridle

Cavesson, flash or drop noseband. Figure-8 nosebands are only permitted in eventing (page 27)

Brown or black English or dressage saddle

White, cream, or black saddle pad

Girth to match horse's color

Helmet that meets current safety standards

Hairnet if your hair is long

White shirt and plain stock (see below)

Hunt coat or black dressage jacket

Gloves

Dressage whip (not compulsory)

White, cream or beige breeches or jodhpurs

Black or brown riding or jodhpur boots

HOW TO TIE A STOCK

This bit of the stock goes at the front of your neck

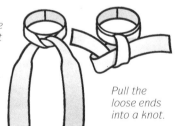

Pull the loose ends into a knot.

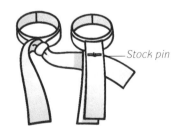

Stock pin

Put the middle of the stock on the front of your neck. Wrap the ends around your neck. If there is a loop on the stock, feed one end through it at the back.

Pass the right end over and under the left. Pull tight. Form a loop with the left end as shown. Pass the right end over and through the loop. Pull into a knot.

Arrange one end of the stock neatly over the other, so the knot is hidden. Secure the ends together with a plain stock pin, fastened horizontally.

BRAIDING YOUR HORSE'S MANE

Braiding your horse's mane for a dressage test makes him look smart. It also helps the judge to see the shape of his neck. Sew the braids and use white plastic tape, as shown below. You will also need some small rubber bands, a needle and thread, and a mane comb. You needn't braid your horse's tail, just make sure it's clean.

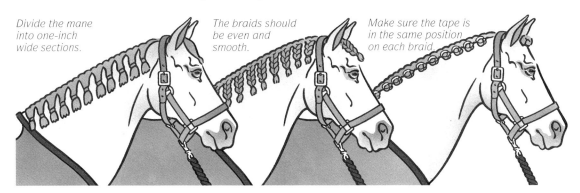

Divide the mane into one-inch wide sections.

The braids should be even and smooth.

Make sure the tape is in the same position on each braid.

Split the mane into sections three-quarters of the width of your comb. Comb each section and fasten with a rubber band.

Take the rubber band off the first section. Split into three parts. Braid them together. Sew the end of the braid to secure it.

Fold the braid under twice. Sew it into place. Wrap white plastic tape around the end of the braid. Make one braid from the forelock.

ADVANCED DRESSAGE

In upper-level dressage, riders use dressage saddles and double bridles. Dressage saddles have long, straight saddle flaps. The girth tabs are also long, while the girth is short, so that the buckles do not sit under the saddle flaps. This helps the rider to keep his or her legs close to the horse's sides.

Double bridles have two bits, and two sets of reins. They give the rider more control over the horse's action.

Top hat

Rider's number tied on bridle

This advanced dressage rider is competing in an international competition.

Shadbelly-coat

Dressage saddle

White saddle cloth showing rider's nationality

Double bridle

Dressage girth

DRESSAGE COMPETITIONS

As well as being exciting and challenging, dressage competitions are a good way of seeing how your training is progressing. In a competition, you will have to perform a four to five minute dressage test, consisting of various different movements. The best way to find out about competitions in your area is from your local riding school or Pony Club Branch.

WHICH TEST TO ENTER

	TEST	DIRECTIVE IDEAS	POINTS	COEFFICIENT	TOTAL	REMARKS
1.	A Enter working trot rising.	Straightness on center line.				
	X Develop medium walk continue to C.	Smoothess of transition. Steadiness of tempo in trot. Quality of walk with relaxation.				
2.	C Turn right in medium walk.	Balance of turn.				
	H-X-K Walk. Develop free walk.	Quality of walk with relaxation.				
	K Develop medium walk.	Straightness of diagonal line. Smoothness of transitions.				
3.	A Working trot rising Continue down long side to C.	Quality and steadiness of tempo in trot, straightness on long side.				
4.	C Circle left 20m.	Steadiness of tempo in trot. Quality of trot. Roundness of circle.				
5. H-X-F	Change rein, working trot rising.	Steadiness of tempo in trot. Quality of trot. Straightness of diagonal line.				
6.	A Circle right 20m.	Steadiness of tempo in trot. Quality of trot. Roundness of circle.				
7. A-K-E	Working trot rising.	Steadiness of tempo in trot.				
	E Turn right.	Quality of trot. Quality and smoothness of turn.				
8.	B Turn right, continue to A.	Balance of turn. Steadiness of tempo in trot. Quality of trot.				
9.	A Down center line.	Quality and smoothness of turn.				
	X Halt through medium walk. Salute.	Sraightness on center line. Smoothness of transition. Immobility of halt.				

Leave arena in free walk on long rein. Exit at A.

Dressage tests are divided into seven levels: Introductory, Training, First, Second, Third, Fourth, and FEI or International Level dressage. There will be several different tests to choose from in your level. Copies of the tests are available through your pony club chapter or directly through the United States Dressage Federation. Send off to the show chairperson for the class schedule and read it carefully before you decide which to enter. Choose a test that has dressage movements you know you and your horse can do well.

Test sheets

Test sheets tell you:
- The order in which you should ride the movements.
- The marker at which you should start each movement.
- What each movement should be.
- The gait in which you should perform each movement.
- The maximum number of points the judge can give you for each movement.

LEARNING THE TEST

Once you've decided on a test, try to learn it by heart. Some competitions let you have a "reader" who calls out what comes next, but it's better to rely on memory. To help you, draw the test out on paper. Go through the movements in your head too. Imagine how you could avoid possible problems. Practice the movements on your horse, but not always in the same order. If he learns the test, he may try to start the next movement before you reach the correct marker.

Try marking out a mini arena on the ground so you can learn the test by walking it.

ARRIVING AT THE SHOWGROUNDS

Make sure you arrive at the showgrounds in plenty of time, as there is a lot to do before you compete. Settle your horse out of the wind, in the shade if it is hot. Leave someone experienced in charge, while you go and check in with the secretary. Find out which arena you will be competing in and confirm your number and start time. Also find out where you can warm up (see page 28).

It's a good idea to watch some of the other competitors in your class, as you may pick up some useful tips.

EVENTING COMPETITIONS

Eventing competitions give you a chance to practise your jumping skills.

You could also enter an eventing competition, which includes cross-country and show jumping as well as dressage. Eventing requires all-around skills and stamina from riders and their horses. Your dressage test is marked normally (see page 29), then converted into penalty points (so the lower your score the better). Your show jumping and cross-country scores are added to your dressage score. The rider with the lowest overall score wins.

RIDING A TEST

When you ride a test, your performance will be watched closely by the judge. He or she will usually sit behind the C marker. The arena will be marked out by low white boards, and it may have tubs of flowers around the outside. Make sure your horse is familiar with these things before you take a test so that he doesn't "spook."

WARMING UP

Before the test begins, you must warm up or school your horse. This makes sure that his muscles are supple and that he is concentrating properly. The amount of schooling he will need depends on his temperament. An easygoing, placid horse will need about twenty minutes, while a lively, excitable horse may need much more. Bear in mind the weather too. You'll have to warm him up for longer on a cold, windy day. Begin your warm-up session by walking him on a long rein before you move on to any trotting or cantering work.

Leg wraps can be worn during warm-up, but not for the test.

Rules for the warm-up ring

- Let other people know you're about to enter the warm-up area by calling out "I'm coming in."
- Walk your horse on the inside track. The outside track is for faster paces.
- Don't halt your horse on the outside track.
- Pass other riders left shoulder to left shoulder.
- Give way to riders doing lateral work.
- If you need to adjust your tack, go outside the warm-up area.

FINAL PREPARATIONS

Aim to finish your warm-up about ten minutes before your test starts. This will give you time to take off any leg wraps or protective boots your horse has been wearing and check his girth. Check your appearance too, then relax for a few moments and collect your thoughts.

RIDING THE TEST

When the rider before you finishes his or her test, start to ride around the outside of the competition arena. When the judge is ready for you to start, he or she will ring a bell or sound a whistle. Tests start at the A marker and finish with a salute to the judge. When you've finished the test, walk your horse back to the A marker, where you should leave the arena.

Tips for the test
* Concentrate hard on what you are doing.
* If a movement goes badly, don't panic, just move calmly onto the next one.
* Don't rush the test.
* Enjoy the movements you do well.
* Make a fuss of your horse after the test.

This rider is saluting correctly. Ideally, her horse should be in a square halt (see page 13).

Saluting
* Halt at the correct marker.
* Look towards the judge.
* Put your reins and whip (if you have one) in one hand (usually the left).
* Drop your other hand down with the back of your hand facing inwards.
* Nod your head down and up again.
* Count to three before you move off.

HOW TESTS ARE SCORED

The judge gives each movement a mark from 0 (movement not carried out) to 10 (excellent). The rider with the highest number of marks wins the competition (unless it is an event – see page 27). At the end of the competition, you will be given a scoresheet which shows your marks and the judge's comments. The judge will also give you a set of collective marks. These refer to your horse's way of going and your riding skills throughout the test.

In advanced competitions there are normally several judges. They sit inside a judging box.

ADVANCED DRESSAGE

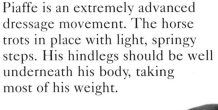

You can learn a lot from advanced riders, whether you go to see them at a show, or watch them on the television. Advanced dressage horses have a high degree of collection (see page 16), enabling them to perform the most difficult dressage movements, some of which are described below.

PIAFFE

Piaffe is an extremely advanced dressage movement. The horse trots in place with light, springy steps. His hindlegs should be well underneath his body, taking most of his weight.

The Piaffe is considered the highest level of obedience and collection, because the horse must trot in place.

The horse should keep his legs moving in a regular trotting rhythm, with a clear moment of suspension between each step.

The toe of the foreleg should be above the fetlock joint of the other foreleg.

PASSAGE

Passage is a very dramatic movement to watch. The horse springs forward in a slow, dancing trot. The moment of suspension between each stride is long and the

horse's steps are high. Passage should be a smooth movement showing the horse's contained energy. Any jerkiness is considered a serious fault.

Horses who can perform passage will have reached the highest level of obedience and collection.

FLYING CHANGES

A flying change involves the horse changing his leading leg in canter, during the moment of suspension (see page 8), rather than through walk or trot. Flying changes are a real challenge to both the horse and the rider because they require split second timing. The rider must give clear, firm aids at exactly the right moment, while the horse must understand instantly what he is being asked to do.

This horse and rider are beginning to work on flying changes. They need to keep the same rhythm and speed.

CANTER PIROUETTE

In canter pirouette, the horse canters around his hindlegs in a half or full circle, without moving forward. The horse should take high, collected steps, and his hindquarters should be visibly lower than his haunches. Canter pirouettes are extremely hard work for a horse, so he needs to have well developed muscles and excellent balance. The horse should keep the correct sequence of footfalls and a steady rhythm as he carries out the canter pirouette.

This horse and rider are performing a canter pirouette in the World Equestrian Games.

A full canter pirouette should be completed in five to seven steps.

INDEX

With thanks to Holly Acuta and Polly, Sally Crisp and Top Gun, Ciara
Gourley and Nula, Kylie Holland and Cnapaton Rosewood, Tarn
Holland and Princess Leya, Sophie Hyde and Moonlight Trickster,
Joe Parker and Harry Houdini.